Franklin's Pumpkin

From an episode of the animated TV series *Franklin*,
produced by Nelvana Limited, Neurones France s.a.r.l. and
Neurones Luxembourg S.A., based on the Franklin books
by Paulette Bourgeois and Brenda Clark.

Story written by Sharon Jennings.
Illustrated by Sasha McIntyre, Robert Penman, Jelena Sisic
and Shelley Southern.
Based on the TV episode *Franklin's Pumpkin*, written by Brian Lasenby.

 ™ Kids Can Read is a trademark of Kids Can Press Ltd.

Franklin

Franklin is a trademark of Kids Can Press Ltd.
The character of Franklin was created by Paulette Bourgeois and Brenda Clark.
Text © 2004 Contextx Inc.
Illustrations © 2004 Brenda Clark Illustrator Inc.

Kids Can Press acknowledges the financial support of the Government of Ontario,
through the Ontario Media Development Corporation's Ontario Book Initiative;
the Ontario Arts Council; the Canada Council for the Arts; and the Government
of Canada, through the BPIDP, for our publishing activity.

Published in Canada by
Kids Can Press Ltd.
29 Birch Avenue
Toronto, ON M4V 1E2

Published in the U.S. by
Kids Can Press Ltd.
2250 Military Road
Tonawanda, NY 14150

www.kidscanpress.com

Series editor: Tara Walker
Edited by Jennifer Stokes
Designed by Céleste Gagnon

Printed in China by WKT Company Limited

The hardcover edition of this book is smyth sewn casebound.
The paperback edition of this book is limp sewn with a drawn-on cover.

CM 04 0 9 8 7 6 5 4 3 2 1
CM PA 04 0 9 8 7 6 5 4 3 2 1

National Library of Canada Cataloguing in Publication Data

Jennings, Sharon

Franklin's pumpkin / Sharon Jennings ; illustrated by Robert Penman,
Sasha McIntyre, Jelena Sisic, Shelley Southern.

(Kids Can read)
The character Franklin was created by Paulette Bourgeois and Brenda Clark.
ISBN 1-55337-495-9 (bound).   ISBN 1-55337-496-7 (pbk.)

I. Penman, Robert II. McIntyre, Sasha III. Southern, Shelley IV. Sisic, Jelena
V. Bourgeois, Paulette VI. Clark, Brenda VII. Title. VIII. Series: Kids Can read (Toronto, Ont.)

PS8569.E563F725 2004   jC813'.54   C2004-901108-1

Kids Can Press is a *l'O*r*u*s™ Entertainment company

Franklin's Pumpkin

Kids Can Press

Franklin can tie his shoes.

Franklin can count by twos.

And Franklin can grow

a really, really big pumpkin.

This is a problem.

What will Franklin do

with a really, really big pumpkin?

One morning, Franklin walked

to Beaver's house.

Beaver was watering her cherry tree.

"Mmmm," said Franklin.

"Can I eat some cherries?"

"No!" cried Beaver.

"These cherries are for a pie.

I want to win a blue ribbon

for the best cherry pie at the Fall Fair."

"Okay," said Franklin.

"But I want a slice

of that pie!"

Franklin walked to Bear's house.

Bear was watering his blueberry bushes.

"Mmmm," said Franklin.

"Can I eat some

blueberries?"

"No!" cried Bear.

"These blueberries are for a pie.

I want to win a blue ribbon

for the best blueberry pie

at the Fall Fair."

"Okay,"

said Franklin.

"But I want a slice

of that pie!"

Franklin walked home.

He went out to his garden.

Birds had eaten

the raspberries.

Worms had eaten

the apples.

And Harriet

had eaten

the strawberries.

Then, Franklin found a vine.

He followed it through the garden.

He followed it around the shed.

And there, behind the wheelbarrow, was …

… a really, really big pumpkin!

"YIPPEE!" shouted Franklin.

"I can make a really, really big pumpkin pie for the Fall Fair! Maybe I will get a blue ribbon!"

Franklin did not tell his friends

about his pumpkin.

Every day before school,

Franklin watered his pumpkin.

Every day after school,

Franklin measured his pumpkin.

It got bigger

and bigger

and bigger.

15

One day, Franklin couldn't keep

his secret a secret any longer.

He asked Beaver to come over.

"Look, Beaver," he said.

"Look at my really, really big pumpkin."

"What is it for?" asked Beaver.

"The Fall Fair," said Franklin.

"I want to get a blue ribbon

for the best pumpkin pie."

Beaver laughed.

"This pumpkin will not make the best

pumpkin pie," she said.
"The best pumpkin pie
pumpkins are very,
very small."

Franklin frowned.

Franklin thought and thought.

He asked Bear to come over.

"Look, Bear," he said.

"Look at my really, really big pumpkin."

"What is it for?" asked Bear.

"The Fall Fair," said Franklin.

"I want to get a blue ribbon

for the biggest pumpkin."

Bear laughed.

"There is no blue ribbon

for the biggest pumpkin," he said.

"This year, the blue ribbon is

for the biggest zucchini."

Franklin frowned again.

Finally, it was the day of the Fall Fair.

Everyone hoped to get a ribbon.

Even Franklin's little sister, Harriet,

hoped to get a ribbon.

"I'm a princess," said Harriet.

"I want to get a blue ribbon

for my costume."

Franklin did not want to go

to the Fall Fair.

He knew he would not get a blue ribbon.

Franklin's mother and Harriet

left for the Fall Fair.

Soon, they were back.

Harriet was crying.

"Everyone was dressed as a princess,"

said Franklin's mother.

"Harriet wanted to be different."

Harriet cried louder.

"Hmmm,"

said Franklin.

Franklin went out to the garden.

He looked at his really, really

big pumpkin.

"Hmmm," he said again.

Franklin called his father.

Franklin's father cut

the top off the pumpkin.

Franklin scooped out the seeds.

Together they huffed

and puffed

and rolled

the pumpkin

up onto Franklin's wagon.

Franklin found paint

and stickers.

He found balloons

and streamers.

He found ribbons

and bows.

Franklin called Harriet.

"Hurry up, Cinderella," he said.

"Your carriage is ready."

"Wow!" said Harriet.

She climbed up on the wagon.

She climbed into the pumpkin.

Franklin pulled her all the way

to the Fall Fair.

By the end of the day,

everyone had a blue ribbon.

Harriet got a blue ribbon

for her costume.

Beaver got
a blue ribbon
for her cherry pie.

Bear got
a blue ribbon
for his blueberry pie.

And Franklin got
a blue ribbon, too.

"Congratulations, Franklin!" said Mr. Mole.

He handed him the ribbon for

The All-You-Can-Eat Pie-Eating Contest.

Franklin tried to smile.

"I don't feel very good," he said.

And so ...

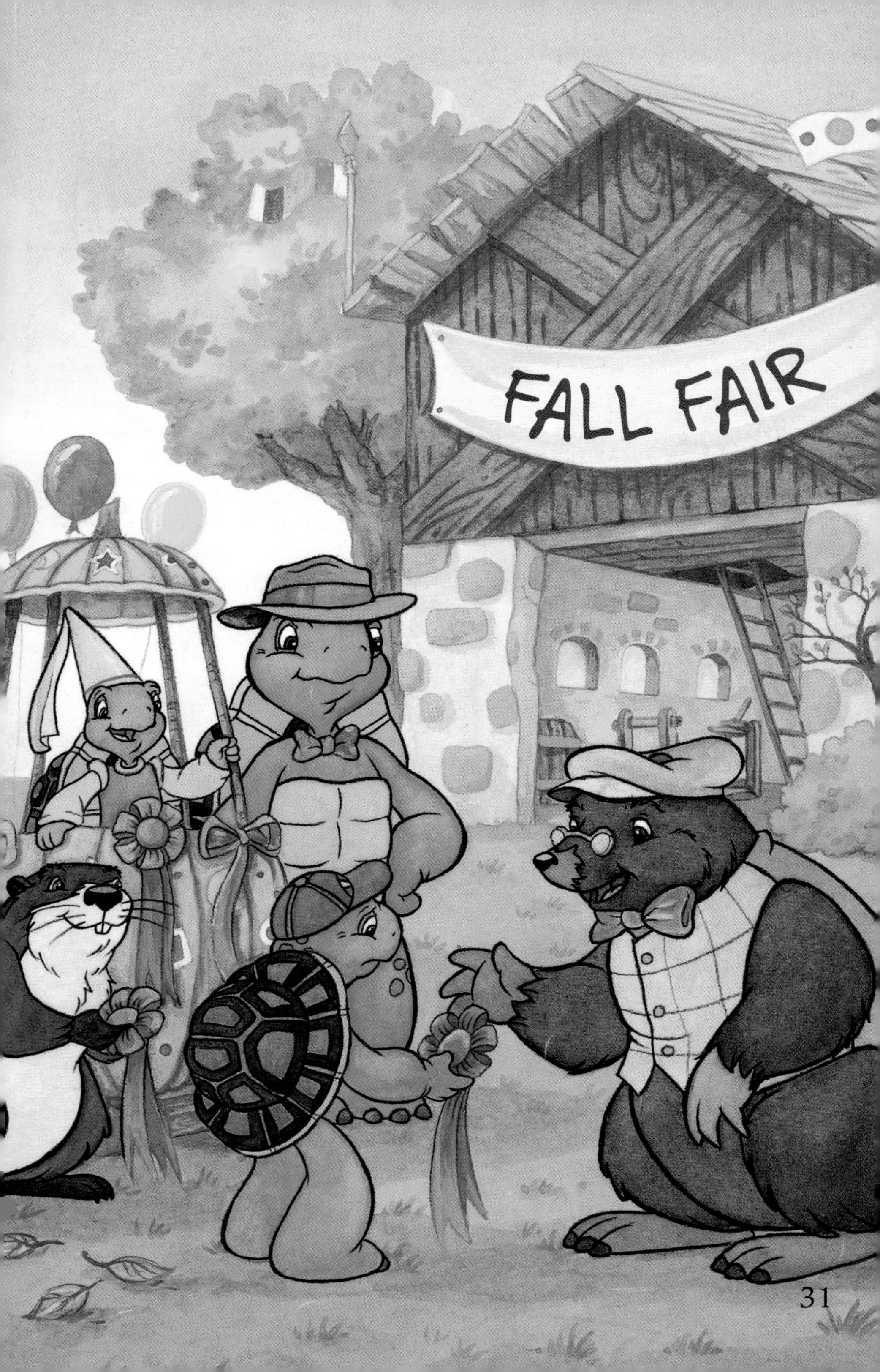
FALL FAIR

Franklin's parents put Franklin

into his really, really big pumpkin.

And they pulled him all the way home

from the Fall Fair.